Bit by Bit

Text by
Shoichi Nejime

Illustrations by
Heather Castles

ANNICK PRESS

TORONTO + NEW YORK + VANCOUVER

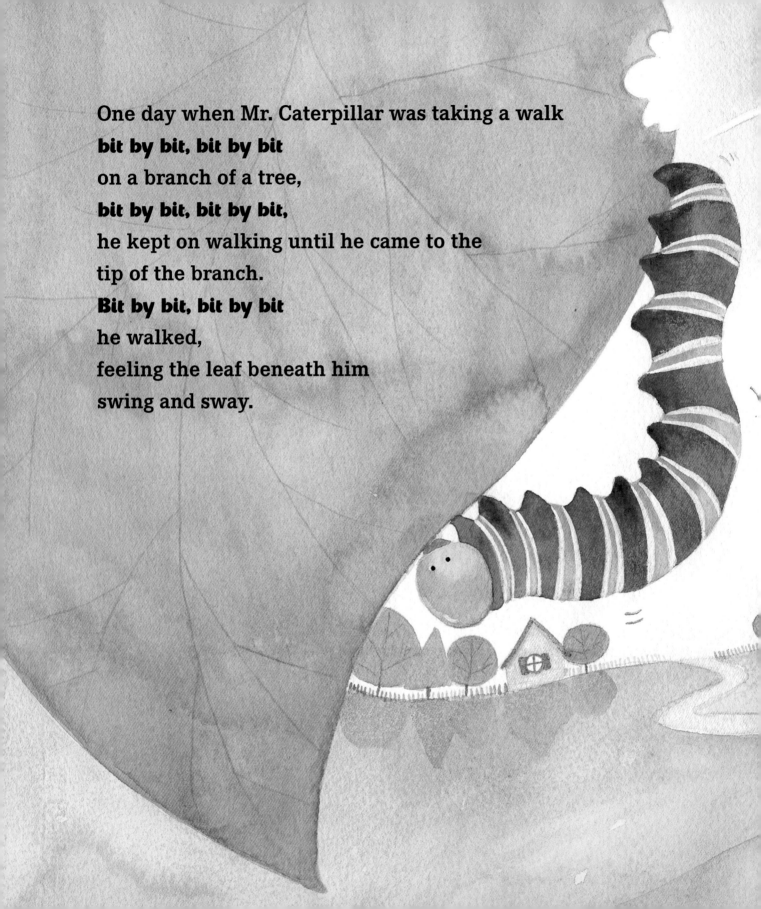

One day when Mr. Caterpillar was taking a walk
bit by bit, bit by bit
on a branch of a tree,
bit by bit, bit by bit,
he kept on walking until he came to the
tip of the branch.
Bit by bit, bit by bit
he walked,
feeling the leaf beneath him
swing and sway.

He was having fun.
All of a sudden a gust of wind swept him off,
and he felt himself float up into the air,
caught in the whirl, turning

over and sideways, over and sideways.

"Ahh…This is it!" he thought.

So he shut his eyes tight and …

...then felt himself hit something firm.
He wasn't sure what it was but clung to it,
then slowly opened his eyes.
He was on top of a gentleman's hat.

The gentleman wearing the hat
with Mr. Caterpillar on top
continued on going, on and on,
swiftly and surely, swiftly and surely.
What a pace he was keeping!

Mr. Caterpillar loved walking on top of big trees
bit by bit, bit by bit,
but he sure did not like being on top of a hat.
It didn't allow him to walk the way he liked to,
bit by bit, bit by bit.
He decided to stay put.
That was when the gentleman suddenly came to a stop.

And then he said,
"My, Mrs. Quick, it has been a while, hasn't it?
And how are you doing these days?"
That was when Mr. Caterpillar got flipped off.

Whoosh.

He gently landed on the shoulder of the
woman's jacket.

Then the woman went on her way,
even faster than the gentleman's pace!
Rushing and hurrying, rushing and hurrying,
she had to get there fast.

Rushing and hurrying, rushing and hurrying,
she walked through the ticket barrier.
She leapt up the stairs.
Rushing and hurrying, rushing and hurrying,
she saw her train.

Breathless, she got on the train.
When she found her seat
she placed her bag on it.
Letting out a big sigh,
she mumbled,
"Whew, I made it!"
And that was when
the train slid out
from the platform.

The woman took her jacket off, complaining of the heat.
"It is too warm, much too warm."

Plunk!

That was when Mr. Caterpillar landed on the seat.

"Oh, good heavens, of all things,
it's a caterpillar!"
The woman swept
Mr. Caterpillar off the seat
with her big, hurrying hand.

"A caterpillar! I want to see!!"

a girl started to shout.

"A caterpillar? Where?"

Many voices could be heard now.
Mr. Caterpillar got frightened by the commotion and
bit by bit, bit by bit
he started to run away.

A tree…
Where can I find a tree?
I want to find a leaf to hide
myself behind.
Where can I find a nice leaf?
Bit by bit, bit by bit.

"There! There he is!"

"Squish him!"

He heard another voice
catching up to him.
A big, black leather shoe
was right behind.

Mr. Caterpillar goes
bit by bit, bit by bit.
He is on the run,
Stretching and shrinking,
stretching and shrinking
away from the leather shoe.

Bit by bit, bit by bit,
stretching and shrinking.
But the leather shoe does not stop its chase.

It casts a dark shadow over Mr. Caterpillar's head.
Mr. Caterpillar pauses and stiffens his body,
saying, "Ahh…This is it!"
when a huge clattering sound is heard.

BONK!

CRASH!

It was some sound, indeed!
And the dark shadow that was over
Mr. Caterpillar's head was gone.
The vending trolley had collided
with the leather shoe!

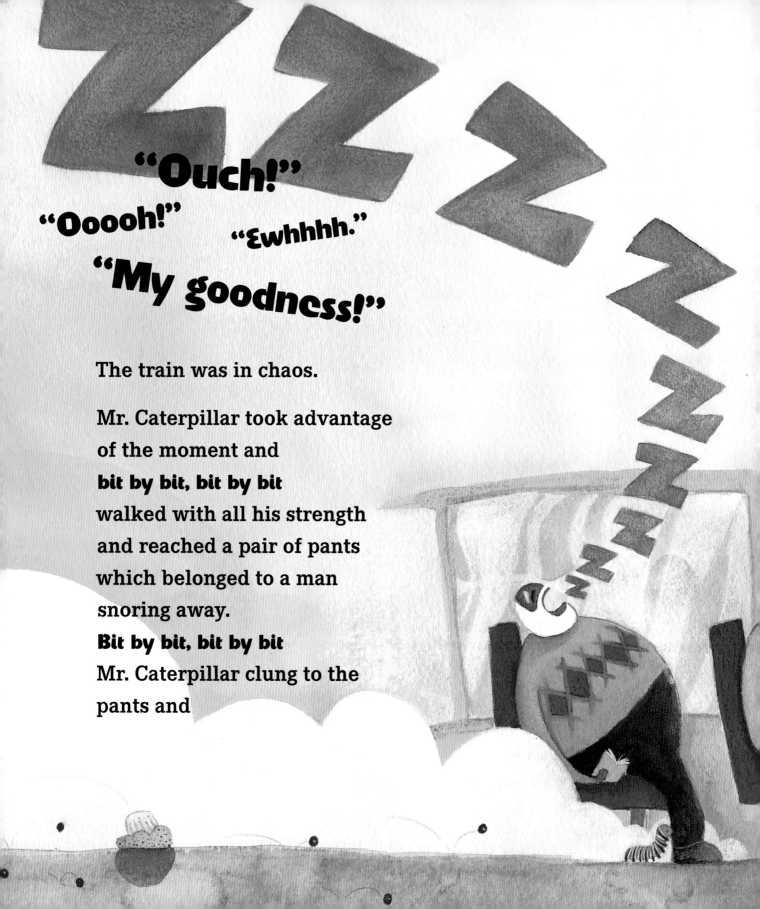

"Ouch!"

"Ooooh!"　　**"Ewhhhh."**

"My goodness!"

The train was in chaos.

Mr. Caterpillar took advantage
of the moment and
bit by bit, bit by bit
walked with all his strength
and reached a pair of pants
which belonged to a man
snoring away.
Bit by bit, bit by bit
Mr. Caterpillar clung to the
pants and

bit by bit, bit by bit
climbed over the folded hem,
bit by bit, bit by bit,
and snuggled himself in between.

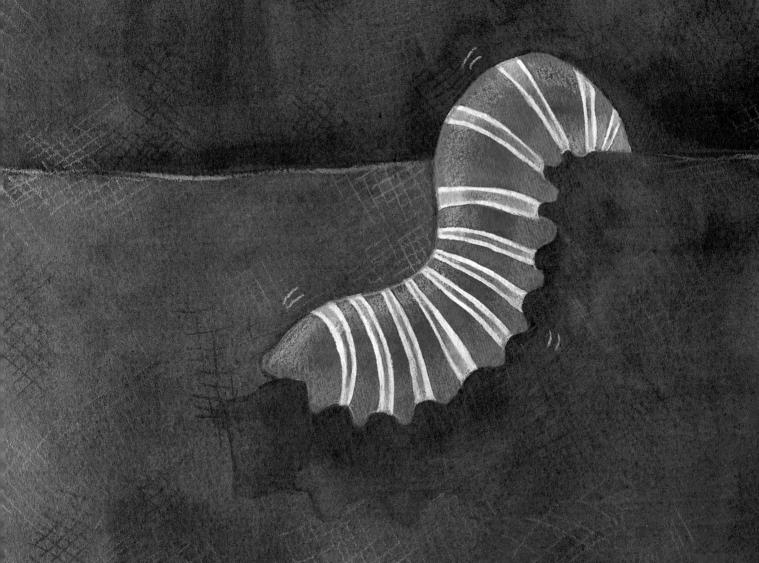

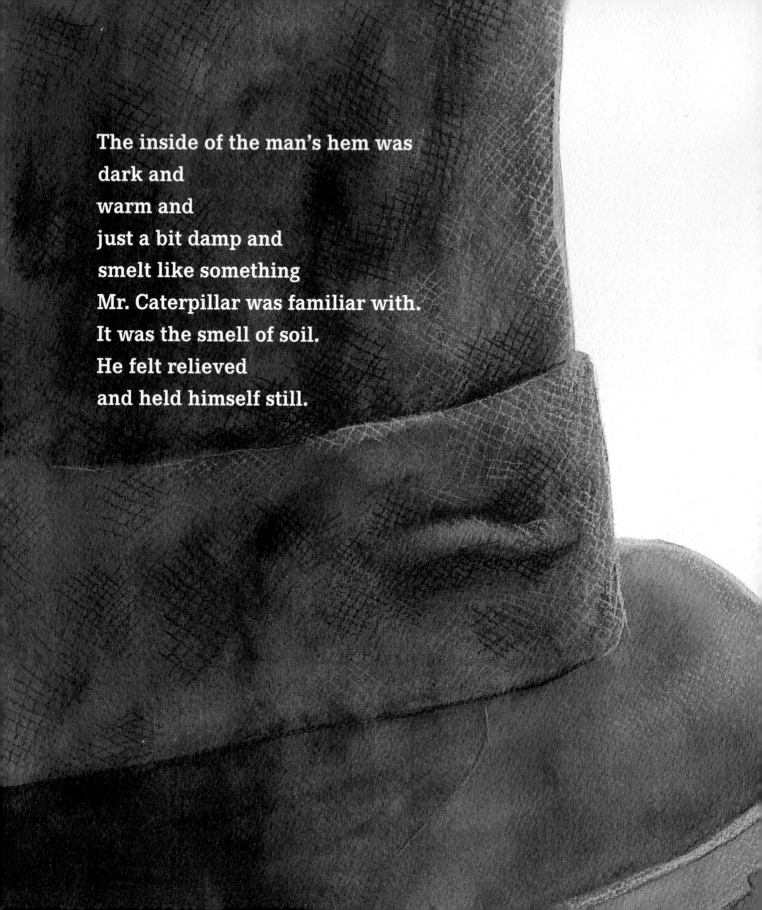

The inside of the man's hem was
dark and
warm and
just a bit damp and
smelt like something
Mr. Caterpillar was familiar with.
It was the smell of soil.
He felt relieved
and held himself still.

Mr. Caterpillar could hear
a child trying to wake the man.
Mr. Caterpillar pretended he was dead
and the man did not wake up.
Mr. Caterpillar knew to be even more careful
when the child said,

"I think I saw a caterpillar go in your pant cuff, Sir."

Mr. Caterpillar held himself still
right against the inside of the cuff.
Then Mr. Caterpillar heard the man
start to snore in a very loud tone.
The child gave up
and walked away.

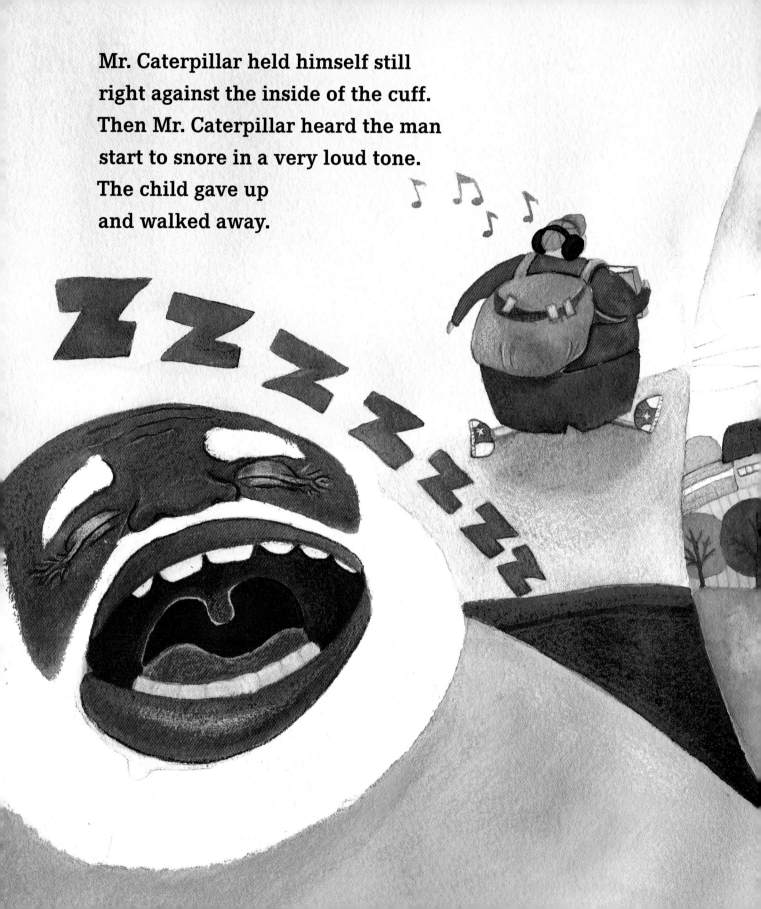

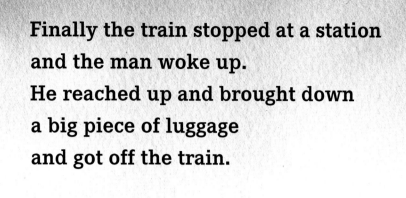

Finally the train stopped at a station
and the man woke up.
He reached up and brought down
a big piece of luggage
and got off the train.

He walked through the ticket barrier
and hopped on a bus.
He got off the bus and started to walk.
The smell of soil was everywhere.

The man finally reached his house and shouted,

"Hello, I'm home."

A woman called out to him,
"Welcome home, how were the grandchildren?"

"They were all wonderful," he replied,
undressing himself.

Getting ready to shower,
the man started to fold the pants
he had taken off when out from the hem
a caterpillar fell to the floor.

The floor was slippery but
Mr. Caterpillar went on
bit by bit, bit by bit
and tried to run away.
The woman saw him and called out,

"Oh no, a caterpillar!"

She flung Mr. Caterpillar
out the window to the garden
where he hit his head
on the bare roots of a tree.

He got a bump on his forehead
and screamed, "Ouch!"
Looking up, he saw a huge tree
standing in front of him.

So Mr. Caterpillar climbed up the big tree
bit by bit, bit by bit.
He kept walking until he came to a branch
bit by bit, bit by bit
where he felt a big leaf beneath him
swing and sway.
He was having fun.

Eventually it grew dark.

Mr. Caterpillar swung back and forth on the leaf,
dreaming of becoming a butterfly one day,
swaying and dreaming, swaying and dreaming,
and then he fell sound asleep.

Text © 2005 Shoichi Nejime
Illustrations © 2005 Heather Castles

Annick Press Ltd.
First published by Fukuinkan Shoten Publishers

We acknowledge the support of the Canada Council for the Arts, the Ontario Arts Council, and the Government of Canada through the Book Publishing Industry Development Program (BPIDP) for our publishing activities.

Copy edited by Elizabeth McLean
Cover and interior design by Irvin Cheung/iCheung Design

The text was typeset in Corporate and Penguin

Cataloging in Publication Data
Nejime, Shoichi, 1948–
Bit by bit / Shoichi Nejime ; illustrations by Heather
Castles. – North American ed.

ISBN 1-55037-907-0 (bound).–ISBN 1-55037-906-2 (pbk.)

I. Castles, Heather II. Title.

PZ7.N434Bi 2005   j895.6'35   C2005-901386-9

Printed and bound in China

Published in the U.S.A. by	**Distributed in Canada by:**	**Distributed in the U.S.A. by:**
Annick Press (U.S.) Ltd.	Firefly Books Ltd.	Firefly Books (U.S.) Inc.
	66 Leek Crescent	P.O. Box 1338
	Richmond Hill, ON	Ellicott Station
	L4B 1H1	Buffalo, NY 14205

Visit our website at **www.annickpress.com**